THE AVOIDABLE ORPHAN

A CHILD OF AFRICA STORY

SHADOWS OVER AFRICA

T.M. CLARK

First Australian Publication 2015

THE AVOIDABLE ORPHAN

Copyright © 2015 by T.M. Clark

Published by Wilde Press

Edited by Creating Ink

Cataloguing-in-Publication details are available from the National Library of Australia www.librariesaustralia.nla.gov.au

ebook © Published 2023 ISBN 978-0-6459192-0-2

First Paperback Edition 2023 ISBN 978-0-6459192-1-9

GENERAL FICTION

This is a work of fiction. Names, characters, places, and incidents are either the product of the author's imagination or are used fictitiously, and any resemblance to actual persons, living or dead, business establishments, events, or locales is entirely coincidental.

This book is written in English as used in Britain and Australia. It has not been Americanised.

DEDICATION

For my Shaun, as always.

Thank you to:
Dave & Pat Tarr for your baby elephant that inspired part of this story.

CHAPTER 1
THE ORPHAN

'I'll get that,' Rodger de Jonger said, putting down his white linen napkin next to his plate and pushing his chair away from the table where he'd sat with his two daughters. He walked from the dining room and down the passage to where the telephone hung on the wall. He lifted the black handset as it rang its last long sound, two shorts and two longs, his call sign on the party line.

'Hello,' he said into the receiver.

'Rodger, it's Leslie. How are you doing?'

'Nice to hear from you,' he said, hearing a faint click on the line. Old Mrs Humphries had picked up and was listening in as she always did, especially to late night calls.

Rodger ran a hand through his hair. If Helene had been here, she would have told Mrs Humphries to get off the line, that the call had nothing to do with her. But she wasn't here, hadn't been for months. He'd never hear his wife tell the old duck off again.

'I'm good thanks,' he said to Leslie. *Managing*. 'To what do I owe the pleasure?'

His friend Stephen had been the head ranger at Chizarira until Independence. It had been one of the first to negotiate with the local chief to build a safari lodge on the bank of Kariba—near Binga. Stephen had moved there with his wife, Leslie, and toddler Peta. Ten years ago, they had welcomed Joss into their world at almost the same time that Helene had given birth to Courtney, their youngest daughter. The women had already been friends, and after that, their friendship had strengthened—all the way to the end.

'I'm sorry for calling so late, but I need your help,' Leslie said, pulling him away from the pain raging in his chest.

'What happened?' Rodger asked.

'Joss brought home a baby elephant, and Stephen's still in Durban for that travel expo.'

'A baby jumbo?' Rodger turned his back and leaned against the wall, twisting the cord around his finger, then unwinding it again. 'Why am I not surprised?'

'You know your daughters would've done the same.'

'I know. Peas in a pod, those kids. How small are we talking?'

'Small. About a metre at its shoulder. It's taking calf formula from the bottle I used to nurse the Kudu calf a few months back.'

'Where's its mother?' Rodger asked.

'No idea. There've been so many fires in the Chizarira and Chete areas recently. There was also a shootout up in the hills a few days ago. They could've been separated by either.'

Rodger looked at the ceiling. There had been reports of poachers at Chizarira the day before yesterday. It was possible they might have moved west into the Chete Safari area. The problem with uncontrolled fires burning into the national park, and into the safari areas, was as bad as always. It was so dry, the small amount of rain they'd received had not broken the drought, and the veld went up in flames at any spark.

'Bongani said he was hunting with Joss up in the forest area near the Chete border when they saw a bateleur eagle circling, so they went to investigate and found the baby lying there. He was still in the TTL—'

The Tribal Trust Lands, good thing they were within those boundaries and not in the park. 'How can I help?' Rodger asked as he sat on the chair in the passageway ... Helene's favourite chair, complete with her patchwork cushion that said "*home sweet home*". She was the one who had liked to yabba-yabba on the phone for hours, not him. He hadn't had the heart to move it though. It still belonged in "her" house. This place had always been her domain.

'I'm going to need your help to negotiate with ZimParks to get permission to keep it while we try and get it to an age where it can be reintroduced back into a wild herd,' Leslie said. 'I can't have a full-grown elephant hanging around the lodge now.'

'Are you crazy? Do you know how much work a baby elephant is? They're so difficult to nurse …'

'I can only imagine. But this baby wants to live, and my son is desperate to give it a fighting chance. I know that the Parks Board gave elephant babies to farmers in Matabeleland after the last cull, so it can be done.'

The culls of the 80s had been a sad necessity. To avoid overpopulation and prevent the destruction of the habitat, whole herds had been gunned down. No one was willing to let the elephants starve like they had in Tsavo National Park in Kenya. The Parks Board had tried to save some of the babies that weren't milk dependent but were still young enough to adapt to human contact. Those babies had been distributed to game farms and new safari areas.

'The elephants we gave to the farmers were at least two years old, able to survive on cubes and browsing. We had to shoot the older ones, around three and a half years old. The cull was too traumatic for them. We had to put down the very young too. In the end, it's kinder,' Rodger said.

'I don't want you to shoot my elephant!'

'It might come to that. It sounds too young.'

'Well, this one needs to be cared for. Surely, we can make a try. It's Joss…'

'It's always Joss who brings you the strays.'

'Too true.'

'What if I come over in the morning and take a look?' Rodger said.

'Thank you but leave your hunting rifle at home. You're not shooting this elephant. If Courtney knows you're coming, she'll want to come too—and she couldn't cope with that either. Bring Peta if she's home. It's been a while since I saw her.'

'Peta got home a couple of days ago. I'm sure she'd love to come along to say hi.'

'Is she enjoying varsity?' Leslie asked.

'What do I know? I'm just the dad.'

The fact that he'd begged her to come home sat heavily in his heart. Peta wanted to stay clear of him, and his moods. Rodger knew it, and understood. But didn't like the idea of his baby girl being almost too independent to need him anymore—that he might lose her entirely now that her mum was gone. That he might never see her …

He took a deep breath as Leslie asked, 'Who can I call for help?'

'You're going to put in the effort even if it means a slow death for the animal?'

'I have to at least *try*.'

Helene would've pressed him to try and save the baby, just like Leslie. It was Helene who'd always nursed the reserve babies along, healed the sick animals. She'd been more of a veterinarian and animal carer than he ever would be. He was the ranger—the one who made the tough decisions, like which herd of elephants to cull when the need arose. The one who had to hunt rogue bulls or lions when they wandered into the *kraals* near the border and became man-killers. The one who was constantly settling human and animal disputes.

He didn't have *time* to be soft.

That'd been Helene's job.

But now she was gone, and not only was there a huge void in his life but in his working environment. She'd been so much part of his team. Once he'd been head ranger of Matusadona National Park—now, a few years after Independence, he worked for them as a consultant. He still lived within the game reserve. Only now he answered to Africa Wildlife In Crisis, an international wildlife monitoring charity that worked alongside the world bank and governments to try to manage the wildlife of Africa with transfrontier conservation areas.

He was torn between the practicality of destroying this elephant, and trying to save it.

Could trying to save this baby turn into something more … something truly special that might help him bond again with Peta and Courtney? If they worked together to help this baby survive, perhaps the fragile relationship between father and daughters would also survive.

Leslie's voice cut into his thoughts.

'Rodger, you there?'

'There's a game ranger in Kenya,' he said, 'who started saving babies about ten years ago. Give me a few hours to find him.'

'Are you going to come tomorrow?'

'Yes. But let's not get ahead of ourselves on the outcome.'

'Any local names you can give me? Farmers who at least tried?'

'I'll look in my office files. But like I said, the ones we gave away and survived were older.'

'Should I call in a vet to check it over, make sure she's okay?'

'I'll contact Jeff, the state vet. Arrange to meet him with you tomorrow at your lodge.'

'Thanks,' Leslie said. 'I'll send Bongani to Binga to meet you at the airport. He can bring you back by boat. It's a smoother ride.'

Rodger rubbed his eyes. 'Thanks. I'll also bring Tsessebe, so it'll be the four of us.'

'The lodge is pretty empty with the start of the rainy season, so fitting you all in won't be a problem.'

'Leslie, it's not that I don't want to give you hope. I could sure do with a miracle in my life now. But if this little jumbo doesn't make it to morning, let me know, okay?'

'I'm thinking we could all use a miracle right now. Bye, Rodger.'

Placing the phone on the cradle, a whisper of a noise let

him know he wasn't alone. He turned to see Courtney standing down the hall.

'Who was on the phone, Daddy?' she asked.

'Aunty Leslie.'

'Is Joss okay?'

'He's fine. She needed my advice about something.'

'Good, because Joss is my bestest friend in the whole wide world, and now after Mummy died, he's my only friend.'

Rodger's heart ached for her. She'd plenty of opportunities to socialise during the week at boarding school in Kariba. But Joss and Courtney chose to stick together. They'd known each other all their lives. It was difficult for anyone to break into their tight little circle.

'So, what about me?' he asked. 'Aren't I your friend?'

'No. You're my daddy,' Courtney said, then turned away to walk back down the hall.

Rodger wiped the tears from his eyes as he followed her.

He sat down at the table and lifted his fork. When he was sure there was no trace of water in his eyes, he looked up at Courtney. Her plate was clean, her dinner finished, but she still sat staring at him. Waiting.

Peta's knife and fork were laid on her plate. She'd left half her food again, but he couldn't bring himself to tell her to eat more. She'd hardly eaten anything since she'd come home, and he could see that her clothes hung on her. He couldn't order her to eat, he didn't want to argue. Their short time together was too precious.

If Helene were here, there would have been laughter and non-stop talking, not the sad silence that had descended on the house since she'd died.

"Talk to them," Helene would've said to him, and he

found his mouth opening, then closing before he said, 'Tomorrow we're going to Joss's to look at a baby elephant he found. Tsessebe's coming too.'

'Joss found a baby elephant?' Courtney asked. 'Does he get to keep it as a pet?'

'We don't know if he's going to get to keep it yet. It's really young. Too young to be away from its mother. We need to go visit and see what its chances are.'

'When I grow up,' Courtney said, 'I'm going to be a veterinarian like Peta, so I can make sure that every animal lives.'

Rodger managed a smile. 'You do that, my angel. You do that.'

CHAPTER 2
THE INDABA

The twin hull catamaran sped through the water making white-washed waves trail behind like a huge motorised butterfly. Rodger smiled as he watched Courtney who sat on the front, her eyes closed, face to the air. He saw so much of Helene in their daughter, it ripped at his heart.

'How much further, Daddy?' she called.

'Only a little way.' he said, looking at the familiar lake frontage of grass and dead trees.

Their trip down in the small Cessna plane he used for his aerial surveys and commuting from Matusadona to Binga had gone well. A quick shopping trip into Kariba, and now they were on Stephen's catamaran heading around the headland and into the river mouth towards the lodge. A far easier route than using the gravel road that snaked its way over impossibly rough and rugged countryside.

After speaking with the people at the David Sheldrick Wildlife Trust in Kenya, he'd wanted to change his position on this plight. That small elephant was probably doomed.

But seeing the excitement in his daughters had made him hold his tongue.

Even one day spent with the elephant was worth seeing them smile. They'd smiled more in the last twelve hours than he'd seen them do in the previous six months.

Looking at Courtney, he saw Helene all over again, with her kind, infectious smile and small mannerisms that she'd picked up, like constantly sticking her long fringe hair behind her ear like her mother.

Peta's excitement had been evident when he'd told them, and he knew he'd done the right thing. She was so much like him. She was the strong one, and at eighteen she showed none of the feminine traits that her mother had tried so hard to instil into her. She still preferred her denims and button-up shirts to dresses and was happiest when she was outside under the African sky. She'd always been so determined to follow in his footsteps, but she knew that being a Park Ranger was now out of the question in the new Zimbabwe. Most of the government posts had been allocated to black Zimbabweans after Independence. So she'd opted to enrol at the University of Pretoria in South Africa to get her veterinary degree.

She'd only been there six months when they'd lost Helene. And he was so scared he would lose Peta now, too. After the funeral, she'd simply bottled up her emotions deep inside and continued on as if Helene had been dead for years. Having so much distance between them hadn't helped. He was looking forward to these holidays, to spending time with her again.

'Look, Daddy! I can see the lodge on the hill,' Courtney said.

'Yes, honey. We're almost there,' he said, bringing his

thoughts back to the present, focussing his eyes on the boxes packed on the deck. Staple supplies to take to the lodge and all the tins of nutritious S26 baby formula that the Spar in Kariba had in stock. Tins and tins of coconut milk he'd found at the Asia Corner market store had been added to the supplies after the Kenyans had told him what to feed the baby elephant. Courtney had found some chocolate, and despite its exorbitant price, he hadn't been able to say no to her when she picked up enough for a picnic in her excitement to see her friend Joss. Allowing the moment of overindulgence.

Peta hadn't picked up anything. Instead, she'd waited patiently while her sister's effervescent excitement had spilt over to everyone else.

Except her.

Rodger looked at the horizon again, at the lodge on the hill, and smiled. His friend had had such foresight to get into the tourist boom so early. He watched for hippos now that they were closer to shore. Many a boat had been toppled by the animals; they were difficult to see in the water as they wallowed in the shallows.

Bongani powered down the throttles and slowed the catamaran. The long jetty, which stuck out into the water, was made from the local mopani trees, as the wood could withstand the scorching sun when the water level was low, like now, as well as flood waters when the rain began in earnest. Old car tyres hung from the side, creating a crash barrier for the boats, saving their precious gel coats, and protecting the wooden structures from the impact caused by the poor docking skills of many of the skippers who used it. Two wheelbarrows waited at the top of the jetty, but no people. Three of the lodge's large houseboats were moored in the shallows, and a speedboat—bearing the lodge's name —was docked on the other side of the jetty.

Bongani lined up the boat with the jetty and slowly motored forward. He put the engine into neutral and came to a stop next to the dock. Tsessebe jumped out of the boat onto the jetty, rope in hand, and quickly tied it up to the stump. The engines went silent as Bongani shut them down.

The heat immediately pressed down on the passengers.

Rodger passed Tsessebe the weapons first, his Merkel 470NE rifle and older .303mm, both in their carry cases.

Peta jumped nimbly out.

Rodger stepped off the back deck onto the dock and turned to hold his hand out for Courtney. She placed her hand in his, and jumped, landing safely next to him.

'The Madame, she is waiting for you by the house,' Bongani said. 'I will bring the supplies.'

'Tsessebe, you can help. We'll see you up there,' Rodger said as he took his rifle bags from Tsessebe and shouldered them. 'Come on girls, let's go visit an elephant.'

With Courtney's hand still in his, Peta fell in step behind as they walked along the jetty and up the stairs to the lodge, and past it to the house.

As they opened the small gate leading to the homestead, two Rhodesian ridgebacks bounded towards them, barking and growling. Doing their job of protecting the private residence.

'Heal,' Leslie called, and the two dogs bounded back to her. A third dog had stayed close to her the whole time.

'Hello, Leslie,' Rodger said, leaning in to kiss her cheek. 'You're missing one. Did you lose a dog recently?'

'Ringo is with Joss and the elephant,' Leslie said. 'Hello girls.'

'Joss got an elephant? For real?' Courtney asked, while hugging her aunt. 'I thought maybe dad was pulling my leg.'

'Joss did find an elephant,' Leslie said, down on Courtney's level as they hugged. 'Why don't you and Peta go have a look? They're in the stables.'

Courtney pulled out of Leslie's embrace and jumped up and down on the spot, waiting for her sister.

Leslie put her arms out to Peta.

'Hello, Aunty Leslie.' Peta gave her aunt a hug, but it was quick, and she stepped away.

'Come on, Peta,' Courtney called as she took off towards the stables.

Peta followed at a more sedate pace.

'I see the Beatles are as protective as ever,' Rodger said, using the collective nickname for the dogs.

He hugged Leslie tightly. She was the one lady in the area who no one would ever attempt to mess with. Her four dogs were as vicious as well-trained police attack canines; her constant companions while she ran her lodge or visited the small village nearby where they sourced labour.

But she was also loved in the area by all. She was renowned for helping the animals and saving those that would usually have died. The local population had worn a path from their village to the lodge with their donkey carts through the bush. Stephen had eventually constructed rough roads to the Chete Safari area where the path had been.

'It's good to see you, Rodger,' she said.

He stepped back. 'I spoke with Anton. Do you

remember he worked with the baby elephants after the culls? He's the head ranger at Matusadona now. I told him about the orphan and asked him to get you the permission needed to keep the elephant if it lives.'

'And?'

'He said yes. You nurse it through the hard part, and he's happy for you to try and integrate it. He doesn't hold out much hope though, but he won't be coming and confiscating the animal.'

'That's great news!'

'I bought some of the supplies we spoke about this morning. The boys are bringing them up now,' Rodger said.

'It's good that you brought Tsessebe.'

'Do I ever go anywhere without him? He's my right-hand man.'

Leslie smiled. 'I know. The catamaran made good time with five of you and supplies.' She linked her arm through his, and they walked at a down the path towards the back of the homestead area.

'She's a beauty. She glided over like a water skimmer,' Rodger said.

'Bongani can tend to speed sometimes,' Leslie said. 'He likes to use both those engines and give them a good workout. Clears all the inner workings, so he tells me.'

'Don't hold that against him. We were happy to get here quickly,' Rodger said.

'Come on. Let's go see the baby.'

As they headed for the stables, one of the ridgebacks pushed himself between them. He didn't growl but bared his teeth slightly with a snarl of his lip at Rodger.

'I see Paul is as protective as ever,' Rodger said.

'Don't mind him. You know he's jealous of any man who comes near me, even Stephen.'

The stables were built against the back of a large concrete farming workshop that stood taller than a typical house. The outside wall was used as the back of the stalls and, though not as tall as the workshop, it had sufficient headroom to accommodate a horse if it reared. The remaining sides consisted of wooden poles forming a fence three tiers high. The same simple style poles slid into place to make up the gates. Six stables in all. One was packed to the roof with hay bales and lucerne.

Rodger never tired of admiring what his friends had created, not only the stables where the horses were kept for tourists to ride, but also a pen for goats, sheep and cattle, which was closed up at night to keep out any predators in the area, like lions, leopards and hyenas.

Peta and Courtney leaned on the gate, watching through the beams of wood, while talking to Joss.

'It's kind of small,' Courtney remarked.

'She's a baby. What did you expect?' Joss said.

The elephant lay in the stable underneath a blanket. Courtney bit the inside of her lip, a tell-tale sign that she was unsure about the situation.

'It's so young,' Rodger said to Leslie. 'Can it stand?'

Joss said, 'Yeah, she's having another nap, and she even peed this morning. Both Mum and Bongani said that was a good thing.'

Joss motioned for the girls to come inside the stable and they looked at their dad for permission. He nodded. Peta climbed through the stable door first then turned to ensure her sister was through. Together they walked over and stood next to Joss. The fourth ridgeback watched, then came over and lay down next to them, his tail thumping on the straw.

'Hello Ringo,' Peta said, patting the dog. She ran her hand over his soft ears and gave him a good pat on the shoulder as he lay there.

Ringo licked Peta's hand then put his nose back down next to the elephant as if to say that while he was happy to see her, he was on nursing duty.

Tentatively, Courtney extended her arm to touch the baby elephant.

The elephant opened its eyes, and followed Courtney's movement.

'She's awake again. Introduce yourself. Ndhlovy loves to smell you with her trunk,' Joss said. On cue, the little elephant put the tip of her trunk into Courtney's outstretched hand.

'She likes you,' Joss said.

Peta knelt down near the elephant, and the little trunk came to her.

The adults stood observing for a while before Rodger took his rifles from his shoulder, propped them up against the stable and then walked to the gate area. Slowly he climbed through the wooden bars and squatted next to the elephant. He let Ringo smell his hand and his arm.

'Hey, Joss. It shouldn't be lying down so much,' he said. 'Is its stomach upset and running?'

'A little. It started this morning after we had a bit of a walk outside,' Joss said.

'Is it a bad smell?'

Joss nodded. 'Oh, yeah.'

'Has it been walking around a lot?'

'Only a little bit. Bongani and Mum said to keep her in here, conserve her energy for now.'

Rodger took off the horse blanket and ran his hands from the tips of its large feet to its trunk, pushing, prodding, feeling everywhere.

Bongani and Tsessebe walked up, each pushing a laden wheelbarrow, and stood silently behind Leslie.

'I can't feel any broken bones, but when a baby elephant gets a bad stomach, it's usually a bad thing,' Rodger said quietly.

He stepped away, and the elephant got to its feet. She went to the toilet, and Peta and Courtney jumped out of the stable holding their hands over their noses.

'Oh man, that stinks big time,' Courtney said.

Rodger laughed.

Courtney tried to stop retching.

'You shouldn't laugh at her,' Leslie said. 'It really does smell bad.'

'I know, but I can't help it. Peta can cope with that smell, but Courtney is so like Helene. Remember, it was me who always changed the nappies when the nanny had gone home for the night because Helene would retch and throw up. She couldn't take strong smells, either.'

Leslie grinned. 'Oh, I remember clearly.'

Rodger got back to the patient. 'This elephant is sick. It needs medicine, something to stop the runs. It'll die if it doesn't stop. I called Jeff this morning. He'll be here as soon as he's finished in Chizarira. I believe that the road from there to here is open, even with the recent rain, so he should get here soon.'

Bongani opened the stable gate. 'Come on, Ndhlovy. Time to switch again while we get this one cleaned out.'

Joss walked the elephant into the new stable a few doors down. The dog stood up, waiting for the command to follow. 'Come on, Ringo,' Joss said.

'Looks like you've done this stall switch a few times,' Rodger said.

'Every time she goes to the loo,' Joss said, 'we switch, and then Mossman cleans the stables and puts in the clean grass.' The little elephant started winding his trunk around Joss's arm and kissing his cheek. 'She's hungry again. Better get the bottle—'

'Wait,' Rodger said. 'This morning Anton and I spent time on the phone with the keepers at the David Sheldrick Wildlife Trust. While they've been unable to reintroduce an elephant into a wild herd yet, they've been successful in keeping the babies alive. They gave me the milk formula recipe it'll need to survive. Apparently, elephants need very fat-rich milk.'

Leslie nodded. 'Her stomach might settle once we start feeding her the right milk.'

Rodger took a tin of S26, a couple of vitamin supplement packets, and a tin of coconut milk from the wheelbarrow. 'Where can I prepare the formula? I need to cook up this oatmeal to add to the bottle.'

Leslie said, 'There's a Cadac two plate set-up next door.'

'I will show you.' Bongani led Rodger to the small tack room attached to the side of the stables that also held their veterinary supplies.

After a while, they emerged with two bottles. Bongani passed one to Joss. 'Here you go. She feeds best from you.'

'Someone else needs to feed it. The elephant should drink from different people so that it doesn't form too strong a bond with one handler. If that handler leaves, the baby will pine, stop eating and die. It's better to share the workaround with as many people as possible,' Rodger said.

'Can I feed her?' asked Courtney and Peta together.

'There are two bottles,' Bongani said.

'You feed her first, Courtney. I'll feed her the next one,' Peta said, giving the first turn to her younger sister.

'Okay,' Joss said, as he passed Courtney the bottle. 'You put it near her mouth, and she'll lift her trunk. Make sure you push the teat into her mouth. That's it. See, she's drinking.'

'That's very good of you, Joss,' Leslie said, 'to give over care of your elephant so fast.'

'I want Ndhlovy to live, Mum.' Joss patted the elephant's shoulder.

Two of the dogs began barking and took off behind the stables. 'Guess Jeff is here. They must have heard his *bakkie*,' Leslie said. She touched Paul's head, reassuring him that he was to stay with her.

Ringo wasn't interested in his brothers running off. He licked at Ndhlovy's mouth where milk dribbled out as if cleaning an elephant was the most important job in the world.

Rodger realised that he was holding his breath. Courtney was laughing, enjoying herself, even Peta was smiling at the elephant and the dog. He dreaded hearing Jeff's professional opinion, knowing that the norm in these situations was to put down the baby.

He couldn't be the one to do it.

Not this time, not knowing how much heartache that would bring his girls.

CHAPTER 3
ANOTHER NIGHT

Night had spread across the sky, following the red and orange sunset in the west. The temperature hadn't dropped much yet, but it was sure to dip later. The Christmas beetles sang their song, and an owl hooted nearby.

'The kids and Bongani have first watch tonight,' Leslie said. 'You sure you are okay with Courtney and Peta sleeping out there?'

'Like I could stop them,' Rodger said. 'I don't think that I could keep them away if I tried.'

'The jumbo's stomach is easing up a bit, a positive sign,' Jeff said.

Rodger helped himself to another bread roll from the middle of the table. 'I'm glad you said we should try to save it. I know we complain about their numbers, but it's still a baby. I'm a bit worried that you don't want to tie it up, Leslie. It could hurt someone when it gets older.'

'I can't do that. I love that a few years back, the Parks Board gave babies to farmers for their safari farms, but I hate that so many of them ended up shackled, and used for elephant back rides. I don't want that for this baby. I want her to go back into the wild. Joss also wants that. Besides, it's different here. We're part of the bush, ideally placed to reintroduce her. We have the elephants coming down from Chete for a visit every now and again anyway, so the wild herds will have access to her. If they choose to adopt her, then so be it. But if she can't go back and stays around here, the locals will get to know her and won't harm her. She'll be safe.'

Rodger looked out at the view from the lodge, his heart heavy. Helene would have loved to have met this baby elephant. They had often visited their friends and sat in this spot, watching the night sky, listening to the forlorn call of the jackal, gazing at the lights of the kapenta boats as they fished in the lake. If the wind blew in the right direction, they could hear the haunting African songs of the Tonga fisherman as they eked out a living from the waters. Sitting close and holding hands after dinner, they would laugh with their friends as their children played board games at the table in the room next door. Rodger missed the physical contact with his wife. He knew that he would never forget her scent, her smile, the feel of her hands.

Those times were over now.

There'd been days in his marriage he'd wondered why Helene had stayed with him in the bush, remote and isolated from everything. But her love for the animals was as big as Africa itself, and he couldn't imagine them ever changing their way of life. He'd known a love greater than all that. When they had first got together, their romance had sparked and blossomed immediately. Helene's mother had told him love like that either burnt out quickly or lasted a lifetime. He was lucky that theirs had lasted and continued to in his memories.

He remembered her devotion, saying he was stuck with her in the bush even after his place as a ranger had been taken away and he'd had to name a replacement. She'd known that he would want to stay close to the land. When Africa Wildlife In Crisis had approached him, the timing had been perfect, allowing them to stay in Matusadona after all.

Anton had been keen to have him remain in the area so that he could still consult on head ranger issues when they arose. Rodger had spent many hours helping him become the good head ranger he knew that Anton would be. Even with Helene always close at hand, his transition into the private sector hadn't been easy, yet they'd managed.

But now, Helene was gone, and the laughter that had echoed over their lives had disappeared.

'So, what do you think, Rodger?' Jeff asked.

'Sorry. I zoned out.' He took his hands from the table and put them in his lap.

'We were drawing straws for the next watch.' Leslie said. 'The kids can stay there all night, but Bongani needs a break. He spent all last night there. Jeff will be checking it every two hours at its feeding times anyway, and he's going to take the ten to twelve shift. Tsessebe gets twelve to three, and you get three to six. Bongani will end at ten o'clock.'

'Sounds fine. When will we know if that antibiotic you gave it is working?' Rodger asked turning to face to Jeff.

'We'll know by morning. It might have been its little body coping with whatever caused it to be left behind by its herd and becoming so dehydrated. It might be having a reaction to the calf formula—I don't know, but by morning we should see its stool firm up. The baby's system's taken quite a beating, even if it doesn't show on the outside.'

Rodger cleared his throat. 'When I spoke with the keepers in Kenya, they said psychological grief can be one of the causes of diarrhoea in infant elephant orphans, so it's important we make a family for the baby. A big family, so she feels she can leave any of us at any time.'

'Hopefully we'll manage that with all of us here.' Leslie said. 'I'll be asking in the village if there's anyone who would like to volunteer their time with the baby. I know that there are some lovely Tonga people who have helped me in the past, especially when I was nursing Stripe, that young kudu we raised. The people in the village have good hearts.'

'It's a good idea to involve the locals, so they know it.' Rodger said. 'It'll make the baby less vulnerable when it gets older. Less likely to be hunted.'

Leslie said, 'Let's get something to drink and go sit out on the deck for a while before I check on the kids. Thank you so much for coming to help with this little elephant and give her a chance.'

She got up from the table. The men pushed their chairs out and stood too. She signalled one of the waiters to serve their nightly beverage outside and moved onto the deck, the men following her out.

Peta watched as Bongani finished moving the lucerne bails around so that the two younger children could sleep closer together in their sleeping bags, while giving Peta some space. They were on the other side. Only Ringo stayed touching Ndhlovy.

'Do you think Uncle Rodger meant Ringo too?' Joss asked. 'That Ndhlovy could get attached to my dog?'

'Perhaps,' Bongani said. 'I have known animals from different species put together early so that they have a friend … a racehorse and a sheep, or a racehorse and a miniature pony. I have seen a cheetah with a dog, and one time, in Bulawayo, I saw a baboon and a hyena that were friends in the wildlife rescue in *Chipangali*. So there is no reason why a dog and an elephant could not become good friends.'

'But Ringo can't live out there,' Joss said. 'He'll be taken by a leopard. And Ndhlovy can't live here forever. She'll get too big. Can you imagine her trying to walk into the dining room for fruit? She'd knock everything over.'

'Very true,' Bongani said. 'But perhaps while she is sick, Ringo can stay with her, keep her company, and there are lots of us here. We are all looking after her. We are her family now.'

'What do you think happened to her mum?' asked Peta.

'I don't know,' Joss said.

'I think,' Bongani said, 'perhaps with the poaching in the area, that she and her mum got separated. That she could not keep up running with the herd and was left behind.'

'Like it was an accident that she was abandoned?' Peta asked. 'That's a nice thought. I don't want to think that her mum left her on purpose. That she gave up on her.'

'Mothers never give up on their babies, no matter if they are still small or adults,' Bongani said. 'I know my mother. Even when she was dying, she begged my brother to try and be better, to make something of himself. She was not giving up on him.'

'And you?' Peta asked. 'What about you?'

'Me? I am the good son,' Bongani said, and he laughed. 'I have a proper job. When she passed, I was already working with Stephen at Chizarira, and now, here at the lodge. I am not a *skabenga* like my brother.'

Peta smiled.

'Your brother is naughty?' asked Courtney.

'Yes, he was bad, so he went to prison eventually. He got caught poaching. He will be there for nine years. In a few years' time, he will come out again. It is a good thing my mother has gone to be with our ancestors. It would have broken her heart to know.'

They were all silent for a while.

'But you know what?' Bongani went on. 'I have my family still. Other than Stephen, Leslie and Joss, I also have my four sisters, and all their children, and although we miss my mother, we now look after each other. That is what family does.'

'I miss my mum,' said Courtney.

Peta stood up and went to her sister, who wrapped her arms around her neck and climbed into her lap. 'I miss her too, Court, but you have me, and you have Dad. Don't ever forget that we are here still and we'll look after you.'

'And Tsessebe. He is not related by blood, but he's always with you both. Part of your family,' Bongani said.

Peta smiled at him. In the faint light of the rising moon, she saw the white of his teeth flash when he smiled too, and she hugged Courtney closer.

'So, I guess we're like a herd, ' Courtney said. 'Our mum might be gone, but the rest of the family is still here. Just as we are making a new family for the jumbo.'

'Only until Ndhlovy can go back in the wild,' Joss said. 'I don't want her to go to a circus or an elephant back riding safari, having people ride her and poke her with sticks. That would be sad.'

'Ndhlovy needs to be strong and survive first, so she needs sleep,' Bongani said. 'We have to stop talking so she can rest, and hopefully, she will get better.'

'Okay, night then,' said Joss as he lay down.

Peta hugged Courtney one last time then tucked her into her sleeping bag next to Joss. 'Sleep well both of you.' She walked carefully back to where her own sleeping bag lay on the bale.

After a time, Peta asked, 'Bongani, do you still miss your mum now that she has passed over?'

'Every day. And as the years go by, the hole in my heart becomes smaller because I remember her and those memories heal. I remember the good times, not the end,' Bongani said.

'I hope that is true, Bongani,' she said. 'Because that's how I feel. That when my mother died, she ripped out my heart and took it with her.'

'Like Ndhlovy, you need time, Miss Peta,' Bongani said. 'Time to heal. And you must remember that your father is always there for you.'

Peta snuggled down on the bales, and eventually, her eyes became too tired to keep watching the elephant, and she slept.

'What are you doing for Christmas, Jeff?' Leslie asked. 'It's only a week away.'

'I'm on call, so I'll probably be having it around Hwange National Park, maybe a few beers with the lion and elephant project team down there. They've organised a

Christmas lunch with their volunteers and the parks staff, so I said I'll join them. But that'll depend on what comes up in the animal world. You never know …'

Leslie smiled. 'Hopefully, it'll all be quiet, and you'll get to spend some time with them. Rodger, you?'

'Nothing definite at the moment. We were thinking of having a dinner at home, but with Helene gone ....'

'Why not spend it here with us?' Leslie said. 'It'll be like old times. The kids will be together; hopefully, the elephant will still be here keeping them busy. You can relax and do a spot of tiger fishing with Stephen. I know that Peta will want to stay here, be with Ndhlovy. She'll probably go back to varsity next year bragging about how she helped Jeff with his examination and helped save an elephant.'

'And so she should,' Rodger said. 'It's not every vet student who gets a chance to practice their profession before they've qualified. I think this might cement her major in large animal husbandry. I'll talk to the girls, see what they think.'

Leslie nodded. 'Other than houseboat charters for Christmas, I only have a few people booked in at the lodge until after New Year, so it could be a week of relaxing. It'll do you guys good to be out of the house, doing something.'

Dragging his gaze away from the stars in the clear sky, Rodger stood up. 'I agree. They've smiled more in the last twenty-four hours than in a very long time. It's going to make it really hard to leave the elephant behind when the time comes. You might end up with us *all* holidays.'

'I think we can manage that, and the other kids will keep Joss out of mischief. Well, Peta will try to keep Courtney and Joss out of mischief I should say.'

When Leslie laughed, Rodger chuckled too.

'So, Jeff, almost ten,' he said. 'Time to take a walk and go check on your patient. I'll come to check on the kids.'

Jeff downed the last of his drink. 'Good idea, I'll grab my bag on the way.'

'I'll come with too, to see how Joss and Ndhlovy are doing. Last night Bongani said the baby woke him every two hours, her little trunk tapping him as if she already knew he would be the one to get the milk bottle. Such an intelligent animal.'

'Hopefully it'll do the same tonight,' Jeff said. 'It needs the nourishment. It's a good sign that it started eating the cubes as well. If we can get a bit of green foliage back into its diet tomorrow, it should start to put on the weight it lost and not look so gaunt. Its bloated stomach should subside. It'll feel much better.'

Leslie packed the cups onto a tray. 'I'll pop these into the kitchen and meet you by the back door.'

Rodger could hear Ringo whine as he climbed through the bars. 'Hello, sweetheart. Have you two had any sleep?'

'Some, in between you guys switching your shifts.' Peta said. 'I told Tsessebe I'd help you with this feed. I can't believe one small elephant drinks so much milk.'

'Me neither, to be honest,' Rodger said. Bending down, he stroked Ringo then said hello to the little jumbo.

Peta went with Tsessebe to make the bottles and soon returned. 'Here, Dad, you feed her this time.'

'Me? No, you can feed it. That's what you're studying for.'

'Dad, you have a turn. She's so sweet. You'll fall in love with her.'

'I already have two girls in my life. I don't need a third,' he said.

'Mum would've fed her.'

'In a heartbeat. This was more your mum's thing than mine. Rescuing animals, bringing them up …'

Peta put the bottle in his hand. Ndhlovy smelled the milk and wrapped her trunk around his wrist, pulling the bottle down to her.

'*Awww*, look. She wants it from you, Dad. No backing out now,' Peta said, helping him tip the bottle and put the teat into the elephant's mouth. 'See. Easy as.'

Watching the elephant baby drink the milk, all the time her trunk wrapped around his hand, Rodger's heart melted.

'Mum would have loved seeing you do that,' Peta said.

'And seeing you and Courtney involved here, too. She would have been so proud,' he said, his throat thick, his voice a little huskier than usual.

Tears blurred his vision and rolled down his cheeks. He sniffed, and as Ndhlovy finished her first bottle, she reached up with her trunk and wiped his tear with the tip. Then she butted her head into him as if reassuring him that she was there and there was no reason to cry.

'Oh, Dad, she's so sweet,' Peta said. 'I hope she makes it.'

'I hope so too, but it's going to be a long uphill climb for her.'

Tsessebe passed him the second bottle, and Ndhlovy drank it as fast as she had the first, then she lay down on her side.

Peta pulled the horse blanket up over the elephant to ensure she was warm and Rodger watched as his daughter softly stroked her little cheek.

'Dad, wouldn't it be easier if we took her home to Matu-sadona with us, then the rangers could all look after her around the clock, and it wouldn't cost Aunty Leslie so much money?'

'If there's to be any hope of her integrating back into a local herd when she's better, the baby needs to stay near where she was found. Anyway, Leslie and Stephen can afford its upkeep for a while, and it would hurt Joss to take his elephant away now. He has such hopes for it,' Rodger said. 'It's great to see you're thinking like that, though.'

'Some days, I still feel like I want to wrap myself into a ball and stay in bed,' she said. 'On days like that, I imagine that Mum's not gone for good. That she'll come back and sit with me in my room.'

'If only life could be so simple. If only we could still reach out and talk to her.' He reached for his teenage daughter's hand. 'She isn't coming back, but on days like that, I'll happily come and sit with you. I love you,' he said and kissed the top of her head.

'I know, Dad, I know.' She hugged him back. 'And you do know that I love you, too, right?'

'I suspected. But it's great to hear you say it. It's been a few months, with your varsity travelling and being away ... I missed you so much.'

'I can defer, Dad, take a year off—'

'No way. You've been working so hard for this. You need to keep going with your degree, and when you come back as a vet, you can work alongside Jeff. Or, I'm sure if we approached Africa Wildlife in Crisis they could find some-thing for you. But first, you need to finish your degree. Your sister and I will be fine. We miss you, *heaps*, but we'll muddle through.'

'Yeah, I know. It was just a thought … You seem so lost without Mum.'

'I *am* lost without her. She was my wife for twenty-three years. I'll always love her, and she left me and our two beautiful girls. I'm sad that I lost my best friend, but now I need to learn to be both your mum and dad.' He paused and then added, 'To be honest … that terrifies me.'

'You? Scared? No way.'

'Yes, way. Shaking in my *veldskoens* scared. I can't run a house like she could. I had to employ Emily as a cook, and even then, we can hardly eat some of the food she puts in front of us. You had that meatloaf your first night home. It was like rubber. She told me she could cook when I hired her, but I fear her cooking might kill us all.'

'She can cook, just not our type of food. She cooks this amazing chopped spinach dish with wild herbs.'

'That's not food.' He thought back. 'Your mum was better at the hiring for the house thing than I am.'

'I'll help Emily a bit now I'm home, show her a few of the dishes Mum's taught me. That might help her.'

'And my stomach.'

Peta shook her head and grinned. He kept his eyes on her.

'You know I can't do the everyday things your mum used to do, like braid Courtney's hair,' he said. 'And I should tell you how things are going at home when you call. Little things, like the paint started to peel off the roof, or a honey badger was in the chicken coop again. I always think I should be listening while you talk about your time at varsity.' He drew in a breath. 'But we need to get used to life without her. As long as we stick together and remember her, we'll be fine.'

She hugged him tight.

'Dad,' Peta said, 'can we stay at Aunty Leslie's while the elephant's here?'

'She's asked us to stay for Christmas, so I'm sure she'll be ok if we stay until New Year, and then we can talk to her if you want to spend more time here after that. How does that sound?'

'Perfect.'

Tsessebe climbed through the bars again. 'All done. Clean and waiting for the next feed.'

'Thanks, Tsessebe,' Rodger said.

Peta crawled into her sleeping bag. 'Stay here with me, Dad?'

'I'm all yours, and not because I've got the shift until six o'clock. I'd stay because you asked even if it wasn't on the roster.'

He saw her smile and wriggled down in her sleeping bag, and then she put her head on his lap instead of the pillow. His fingers toyed with her hair.

'Dad,' Peta said, 'if this elephant lives, what do you think are the chances of it going back into the wild?'

'I have no idea, Peta. No idea. But each day we keep Ndhlovy alive is one more day that she wouldn't have had otherwise.'

Rodger continued to thread his fingers through her fringe, absent-mindedly playing with her hair as he stared out into the night. For a long time, the men sat in silence while the children, dog and elephant slept.

Then a leopard coughed close by, and Ringo growled.

'Rodger, you awake?' asked Tsessebe.

'Yeah. Ever tried to sleep with a ton of bricks on your lap?' he asked.

Tsessebe chuckled.

Rodger eased Peta's head off his legs and took his .303 from its bag.

Tsessebe looked at him, shaking his head.

'I'm not stupid,' Rodger told him. 'It's a last resort. Let's light up this area and make some noise. Hopefully, it'll leave, and we won't even need a warning shot.'

Tsessebe went to the wall and flicked on the switch. A light flickered above the stables, and the fluorescent tubes came on. They heard the generator kick in now that they were pulling power, and the sound broke the predawn silence.

Rodger shook Peta. 'Come on, we need some noise. Leopard.'

She nodded and woke Courtney and Joss.

'What?' Joss asked.

'Does everyone have something to make some noise with?' Rodger asked. 'Joss, wake up your elephant. There's a leopard close by.'

Joss sat next to Ndhlovy. 'Come on. Wake up time. We're going to make some noise.'

Ndhlovy opened her eyes and looked at him. She blinked a few times in the bright fluorescent light then sat up on her haunches.

Ringo growled again.

'Noise time.' Peta lifted a nearby tin mug and spoon. Courtney had a mug and spoon too. Joss had a plate. They all clanged and smashed.

Joining in, Ringo howled, and Ndhlovy jumped up, her eyes all white. Scared. Joss put his plate down and patted her.

'We're scaring away a leopard,' he explained. She didn't move, but she looked at him as he smiled.

'Let's try singing.' Courtney suggested. 'Maybe she won't be so scared of that. *Old MacDonald had a farm—*'

'*E-I-E-I-O,*' they all joined in. The clanging stopped, and Ringo howled again. And this time, Ndhlovy lay back down. Her eyes were still open and alert, but the fear was subsiding.

They sang a few verses until they'd run out of animals to add and were all laughing at the mishmash they'd made of the song.

A light flashed along the path as Leslie and her three dogs arrived.

'I heard you had a sing-song,' she said as she climbed into the stable.

'Please tell me you are armed. We were scaring off a leopard,' Rodger said, 'and you are walking around in the dark.'

'I'm always armed,' she said, pointing at the .9mm pistol on her hip. She raised the thermo flask, and the kids all grabbed their cups and put them forward. 'You want some Tsessebe?'

'I would walk unarmed past that leopard for a cup,' he said.

Soon they all sat drinking hot chocolate from their mugs, listening to the birds. Their noise had woken them a little early. But soon the dawn broke, pink in the sky, with clouds hanging close to the horizon.

Ndhlovy had survived another night.

CHAPTER 4
THE VISITORS

The week had passed in a blur of trips in and out with the re-provisioning for the elephant and ensuring the girls had enough clothing for their stay. Rodger never tired of flying over the green grove of moringa and mopani trees that surrounded the lodge, and was thankful for each day. Christmas presents had been relocated from his home to Stephen's and stashed safely away where the kids wouldn't find them. They had all the S26 baby formula and coconut milk they could get their hands on, which had included a quick flight to Bulawayo for a collection from a ranger who had brought some back from South Africa. They had enough oats to last until the week after New Year, and Jeff would bring up more vitamin supplements when he arrived on Boxing Day.

The early morning sun cast a purple hue over the water as Rodger stood on the jetty fishing. Stephen was next to him, casting off the other side.

'Hey, Bongani, you're late,' called Stephen as Bongani stepped onto the jetty. 'Your rod and bait are waiting.'

Bongani looked at the fishing equipment. 'The fishing will have to wait for another day. Last night, the elephants walked through the village. They upturned the donkey cart. The people—they said the small herd seemed to be searching for something.'

'Might be the baby's herd,' Rodger said.

'Maybe. They did not try to raid the crops,' Bongani said.

'You sure?' Stephen asked as he reeled in his line and prepared to recast.

'The only thing they damaged was the cart. Then they moved out of the village. They were last seen heading this way. My father, he said that this is a female herd, not one bull with them,' Bongani said. 'They are worried that the elephants will return this evening.'

'They haven't arrived at the lodge yet,' Stephen said, 'which means they're still in the bush, or they have turned back towards the Chete area.' He brought in his line, hooked his spinner into the eye of his rod and placed it down on the jetty while he packed up his tackle box.

'Did you tell Leslie?' he asked.

'Not yet,' Bongani said.

'I'll tell her,' Stephen said.

Rodger reeled in his line too. 'Whether it's Ndhlovy's herd or not, those elephants might be coming here. We need to make sure that the kids are not outside and Ndhlovy is safe.' He tossed the leftover bait fish into the water and packed up his rod.

Rodger began walking up the jetty with Stephen close behind. 'When I left them at five-thirty, they were already up and having breakfast, ready to walk her through the moringa trees. They planned to take her to the shoreline.

They have spades to dig a hole so she can have a mud bath. Tsessebe's with them and armed, but I don't like them out there with wild elephants about.'

Stephen placed his rod and tackle box at the base of the stairs. 'Bongani, get ready to go tracking while Rodger and I grab our rifles.'

Later, as Bongani changed direction again, Rodger adjusted his rifle higher on his shoulder. The sun, now fully risen, was heating up the thick bush, and the sweat trickled down his back.

They broke into a clearing right on the shoreline. Ringo bounded up to Stephen, and he bent to give him a pat. Ahead, the kids and Tsessebe were digging a hole on the shore.

'Hey, guys.' Rodger moved closer.

'Dad, come join us. We're digging a big hole to give Ndhlovy a mud bath,' Courtney said. 'We dug it away from the shoreline so the crocs can't get Ndhlovy or us. Neat, hey?'

Rodger smiled. It was so hard not to get excited around the kids with their enthusiasm for the little elephant. 'Looks great, but there's a herd of jumbos on their way. We need to go back to the lodge, put Ndhlovy in her stable where she'll be safe, and get you guys out of the open.'

'*Awww*,' Joss said. 'I was looking forward to having a mud fight with Ndhlovy and the girls.'

'I'm sure you were,' Stephen said, 'and you still can, but later—once the elephants have moved away.'

'Okay.' Joss lifted himself off his knees. He attempted to brush the mud off, but it made streaks on his legs, so he left it there and stepped into the hole to wash his hands before drying them on the seat of his pants. Then he turned to Ndhlovy. 'Come on girl, time to head back.'

The little elephant hesitated, torn between the mud bath and Joss. 'Come on, Ndhlovy,' he said again with more authority in his voice. He tugged on her ear and walked a little further away.

She flicked her trunk and followed, catching up to him in no time, butting her head into his back, causing Joss to stumble.

'She's so much stronger after only a week,' Rodger said.

'Yeah, and look at her face. Like Jeff said, less gaunt. Hopefully, she'll be one of the lucky ones,' Stephen said.

They arrived back at the stables and put Ndhlovy inside. The baby elephant was nibbling on a good shake of cubes when she put her trunk in the air, and sniffed. Then she threw her ears forward even before Ringo began to growl.

'Jumbo, three o'clock,' Bongani said, as he retreated into the stable and closed three wooden poles across the door.

'Quiet, Ringo,' Stephen instructed.

Ringo sat next to Ndhlovy, and while his feet moved in excitement, he was silent.

'Get into the next stable. Give them room in case they come to investigate Ndhlovy. Their unpredictability makes this whole scenario difficult to judge,' Stephen said as Joss and the girls climbed through the wooden poles.

Tsessebe stood his ground near the gate, ready with his rifle to his shoulder.

'I'm set.' Rodger took aim from the next door stable.

Tsessebe nodded and lowered his rifle as he followed the others across the two stalls they had climbed through.

'Please don't shoot the elephants, Daddy,' Courtney said.

'We don't plan to. That's the last resort, only if they charge us,' Rodger said. 'If it's her herd, we'll be lucky. If they aren't, hold your thumbs that they are still interested in her, even though she smells like humans. We can only hope that they don't try to kill her.'

The matriarch of the herd slowly walked closer to the lodge's grounds. Her ears were flapping, listening to every sound. Her feet were sure as she placed each on the ground. Her low rumble vibrated through the air.

Ndhlovy walked to the gate and stuck her trunk out, trumpeting.

The matriarch trumpeted back, her trunk dangling between her tusks. Her left tusk was chipped and green from the bulrushes she'd eaten on the edge of the lake.

Peta inched closer to her father as a second female followed; she only had one tusk on the right-hand side, but she looked as formidable as the matriarch. The third was considerably smaller with short tusks, still not fully grown, and had a slight run in her step to keep up. A fourth even smaller elephant followed, also with short tusks. Last came another huge female. Her trunk smelled everything on the ground as she walked at a slower pace, her tatty-torn ears flapping.

The kids stayed silent, not daring to move.

The elephants' rumble was clearly audible like giant cats purring. Ndhlovy trumpeted again.

The matriarch walked cautiously towards the stable while the rest of the herd waited, never standing still, constantly moving, watching, smelling the air.

'Keep real still,' Rodger said quietly.

The matriarch had reached the stable. She touched her trunk to Ndhlovy's, and the purr became a louder rumble. Ndhlovy tried to head-butt the matriarch before wrapping her little trunk around hers and then unwinding it to touch her face. From the other side, the matriarch did the same and then began to investigate the stable structure.

She inched her trunk over the pole in the gate but didn't try and move it. Her trunk moved to the next pole down, testing it. Then she moved slightly to check the last pole.

Ndhlovy tried to put her trunk in between the matriarch's front legs, looking for milk, but she came away with nothing. The matriarch didn't push her away. Instead, she caressed her with her trunk. The other elephants pushed forward. Now standing either side of the older elephant, they touched Ndhlovy with their trunks.

'They seem to know her,' Rodger whispered.

'Could we be that lucky?' Stephen asked.

The smallest elephant was closest to the humans, and while she was cautious, it was as if she knew there was a fence between them. She put her trunk into the stable and took some of the straw bedding. She put it in her mouth, tasting it. Reaching in again, she took more. The one-tusked female did the same, and soon even the matriarch was eating the stable grass.

Flies buzzed around the elephants, and their ears moved constantly, listening, and cooling them at the same time. The matriarch took her time eating the grass, constantly touching Ndhlovy, as did the one-tusked female.

Rodger took a breath and exhaled slowly, lowering his rifle. Clearly the elephants weren't going to be aggressive, happy to eat the hay and interact with Ndhlovy through the bars. The smallest elephant kept one eye on them, but now that she had eaten all the hay she could reach, she moved slightly closer to eat from the stall the humans were in.

Tsessebe carefully kicked a bit more towards the elephant. 'They are hungry,' he whispered.

One-tusk looked at them and snorted.

Low rumblings passed between them. Once again, the matriarch caressed the baby through the gate, and her rumblings changed pitch.

Ndhlovy head-butted the gate, trying to get out. The stable shook. It had been designed for trained horses, not for elephants.

The matriarch pushed the baby away with her trunk and stepped back.

'Oh shit,' Stephen said. 'She's going to break it down.'

But once again, her trunk reached out, touching Ndhlovy's, caressing the baby. Then slowly she let their entwined trunks pull apart as she backed up, being careful of the roof.

The elephants turned as a group and plodded away. Their communications consisted of rumbling and squeals while Ndhlovy turned in circles inside the stable. She trumpeted sadly once again.

The matriarch trumpeted back but continued on her way towards the moringa grove.

'That was a close one,' Stephen said.

'Why did they leave?' Peta asked. 'Why did they go away and abandon her again?'

Rodger said, 'They're hungry. There have been big fires in both Chizarira and Chete, so the matriarch may be having trouble lactating and knows that we're feeding her, caring for Ndhlovy. Never underestimate the intelligence of an elephant.'

Tsessebe climbed out the stable. 'I'll follow, see where they go,' he said and set off at a brisk trot to catch up and watch the elephants from a safe distance.

Joss climbed through and went to get into the stable with Ndhlovy, but she was agitated, pacing. 'Steady, girl, steady ...' He hesitated on the other side of the wooden structure.

She turned her back on him and trumpeted again.

'She's calling them,' Rodger said, and sure enough, a distant answering trumpet came. But the sound was fading, not coming closer.

Ndhlovy ran at the gate again, hit it with her forehead and then stood still as the timber poles held.

'Bongani, can we get her a bottle? That might help calm her down a bit,' Rodger suggested, and Bongani climbed out the stable to fetch it.

Stephen asked, 'Joss, do you want to give her the bottle or do you want one of us to do it?'

'I'll do it,' Joss said, and he took the bottle from Bongani's outstretched hands and closed the distance to the fence.

Ndhlovy turned and ran towards him, but she didn't collide with the railings this time. She stopped short and put her trunk out to Joss as if realising that there were other beings there, and while they weren't elephants, they had milk. She put her trunk up and over his arm that stretched through the fence. While she drank, he ducked through and stood near her.

She didn't try to push him away, and when she was finished her bottle, she continued to hold onto him with her trunk.

'I think we need to keep her in until Tsessebe tells us where they've got to,' Rodger suggested.

'Agreed. While I would love her to go with them, she needs to get stronger first,' Stephen said. 'Jeff said that she would be okay again and at full strength in two weeks if everything went well. It's only been a week.'

'If they come back and want to take her, you won't be able to stop them,' Rodger said. 'This place wasn't built to withstand elephants.'

'I know. And I hope they do come back, but in another week when she's stronger,' Stephen said.

'I can't believe they left her.' Peta's face was pinched and red, and her voice was tight. 'I thought that elephants had a family thing going. They saw her, touched her and left her all alone.' She strode down the path and away from the group.

Stephen ran a hand through his hair. 'What bit her on the bum?'

'She is afraid of being abandoned too,' Bongani said. 'The first night you were all here, she talked about her mother. About being left alone.'

Rodger studied his daughter's back as she continued on her way down the path. His chest tightened, and his breathing shallowed. His daughter was still in so much pain. Somehow, he had to make her understand that he would never leave her or Courtney, at least not anytime soon.

CHAPTER 5
IT TAKES MORE THAN BLOOD

Rodger stopped by the door and gazed at Peta sitting on the deck overlooking the sparkling water of Kariba, sipping a bottle of Coke, her feet propped on the upright of the wooden fencing. He always liked to think she took after him and tended to forget that his child had become a young woman. Women wanted to complicate everything by over-thinking and being overly emotional. Helene used to be like that, and now Peta was too. Courtney hadn't learned that skill yet, but he knew she would, given time.

Peta looked up, pursing her lips. A sure sign of mixed emotions, either confused or mad. He could never tell which. Her face looked flushed as if she'd recently cried, and his heart broke knowing that once again he'd been unable to shield her from the harshness of the world.

'Is it safe to approach?' he asked.

'Of course, Dad. I don't have an infectious disease because I'm mad,' Peta said.

'At something I did or mad at the elephants?'

'I don't know,' Peta said, and she sniffed.

Rodger walked the rest of the way, pulled out a chair and sat down next to her.

'If you don't know, how am I supposed to be able to tell?' he asked.

She shook her head as a smile tugged at her lips, and continued to look out over the water.

'Your mum used to get that same look, especially when she was mad at me.'

After a long pause, Peta said, 'I'm not mad at you, Dad. I'm mad at Mum.'

'Why are you mad at Mum?' Rodger asked, and he reached across and took her hand in his.

She turned towards him. 'I know it's irrational, but she died and left us, and everything changed. If she'd fought harder, tried more treatments, not given up! Instead, she abandoned us all. And that stupid elephant herd, they did the same to Ndhlovy. They came and saw her, and then left.'

'Oh Peta, come here,' he said, and she stumbled out of her chair and into his lap. 'It wasn't your mother's fault she died. She never gave up. She fought right to her very last breath. There was nothing she could do to stop the cancer. It was eating her, and nothing the doctors did could stop it. The cancer was too aggressive. She never wanted to die. She never wanted to leave us. You knew your mum, she was always a fighter. Think back. Do you ever remember her backing down in an argument?'

Peta shook her head.

'She still left us, Dad. She abandoned us while we still needed her. She waited for me to go away, and then she died. If I had stayed at home, and not gone for my second semester, I could've helped her, done more for her—'

'She was so proud of you going to university. Never

doubt that she wanted you to carry on with your studies. She didn't want her illness interfering with your life.'

'But if I'd been home to help her, she might still be alive.'

'How do you figure that?'

'She said goodbye to me ... and then she let go.'

'Peta, her body gave out. If she could still be here, she would be. She was talking about you coming home in December. About how you would've grown as a person. Every time we talked to you on the phone, she would say how much she loved that you had such passion for your degree and that you were so lucky to have found your vocation in life. You gave her something to look forward to. Your calls would brighten up her day. She didn't let go because of you at all. Her body simply failed her in the end, that's all.'

Still upset, Peta shook her head.

'She'll always be in our hearts,' he went on. 'We have photographs of her, and they will keep her face fresh in your mind, and we have home videos. We can play them, and you can hear her voice. We can watch them as a family when you and Courtney are ready.'

'But it's not *her*, Dad. It's only a picture. A ghost of who she really was.'

'That's true. Nothing is ever going to replace her, and no one will. She was your mum. But you need to understand that she never abandoned you. She's always with you. Every beat your heart makes, she's the small echo you hear in the background.'

'I miss her so much,' Peta said.

'Me too.' He held her in a tight embrace.

'Dad, do you really believe that Mum is still around us?'

'Of course. You should hear my conversations with her.'

'You talk to her?

'Uh-huh.'

'You do know she died, Dad. You were there holding her hand.'

'I remember every second. From the first moment I saw your mum riding that darn horse that bucked her right off, to that last precious breath that she took and gently let go of life, I remember, honey. But I can't let go of her. So, yes, I believe that she's here. still with us, watching over us. She won't leave us. She never did.'

'Dad, don't you dare die on me, okay! Even when I'm really old, like fifty, I'll need you around. Deal?'

He smiled. 'Deal.'

CHAPTER 6
THE GROVE

As the sun sank low over Kariba that afternoon—with the sky red and liquid gold water inviting night to cover it in darkness—Tsessebe ran towards the lodge, in front of the three cows and four goats that were returning from grazing.

'They are coming back!' he shouted. 'The herd. We have about half an hour to get ready, then they will be here!'

Stephen jumped to his feet. 'Bongani, quick, if they are coming back, they haven't abandoned Ndhlovy. Rodger must have been right about the food—'

Leslie grinned. 'That's great news! They haven't abandoned her!'

She jumped up and down and hugged Stephen. Joss threw his arms around his parents and jumped with them too.

Tsessebe was nodding, smiling at the family. 'All day I have walked silently, watching them. They have eaten a lot but they are still hungry. The moringa grove will take time to recover. They have also been eating the bulrushes in the small inlets, the sweet grasses on the edge of the lake. They have bathed in the fresh water of Kariba, and when it was hot, they covered themselves in mud. They seem at ease here. If they were looking for something last night, then they found it today.'

'If we feed them, supplement their food for a little while, perhaps their condition will improve, and soon she'll take Ndhlovy,' Stephen said.

Rodger grinned. 'Don't get too excited—you might land up with elephants who won't move away again, wanting you to feed them all the time.'

Stephen said, 'If they are happy then they won't be destructive, and that's a good thing if they're around the lodge, especially if they're going to stay close by.'

Rodger chuckled as the three men carried the lucerne bales out of the stable and lined them up in a row.

'You think they'll stay, Uncle Rodger?' Joss asked.

'Too early to tell. If they're her herd, they might stay, and if they're not, then we can only hope they'll get used to Ndhlovy and take her in. If she isn't theirs, then they need to adopt her. And to adopt her they have to want her as part of their herd. To take her with them.'

'It would be so much easier if we could just ask them,' Courtney said.

Peta laughed as she carried a bale.

Courtney and Joss grabbed the last one, but Leslie took it from them as they were getting out of the stable and carried it.

Five bales in all.

Rodger and Stephen walked along the line and cut the twine so that it no longer bound the feed so tightly.

'Come on, you guys, everyone into the stables like last time.'

Joss and Courtney walked in and bounced onto their hay bales, Peta sat with her back to the wall, next to her dad, and Tsessebe and Stephen sat next to Leslie, Joss and Bongani.

Ringo was at the gate, whining.

'Sit, Ringo,' Leslie commanded. 'Quiet.'

Ringo sat where he was, his tail thumping on the ground in his excitement, knowing that something significant was happening.

They could hear the matriarch's low rumbling before the elephant walked into the stable area from the back road.

The men had their weapons close by, but unlike the first morning visit, their rifles were not trained on the elephant. They watched as the matriarch walked directly to Ndhlovy, as if knowing that she would still be there. Ndhlovy trumpeted as they greeted one another. The other elephants gathered, stepping around the bales to greet Ndhlovy before going back to investigate the treat. The matriarch ate about half of her bale before she started to test the stable door again. This time, she removed the top pole and let it drop into the stable. Ndhlovy stepped back.

The matriarch used her trunk to remove the second pole posing as a gate.

'That's incredible,' Rodger said.

She removed the third one, and Ndhlovy stepped out of her stable. Her small trunk began touching the matriarch all over.

Stephen got his weapon ready to fire into the air if necessary, but Ndhlovy put her trunk to the matriarch's teats again and stayed there for a moment. Then Ndhlovy moved to the one-tusked cow, and after greeting her, she repeated the gesture looking for milk. There she seemed to find something. The elephants were eating their lucerne slowly as if savouring the taste and making the night snack last.

Ndhlovy decided it was bedtime. She lay down on the floor next to One-tusk, and the matriarch moved closer, as did the third big cow. They were closing ranks on Ndhlovy, protecting their sleeping baby. The other smaller elephant joined Ndhlovy and went to sleep next to her.

'It's going to be okay,' Leslie said to Joss. 'Look how they're watching over her.'

Joss grinned.

'I wish she could still be here for Christmas, Mum,' he said. 'But it's neat to see that she has a real family.'

'What do you think happened that they came and found her?' Courtney asked.

'Maybe they lost her when they ran away from poachers or the fire,' Tsessebe said. 'Maybe they got separated and have been looking for her. Elephants return to mourn their dead, and when they couldn't find her body, they must have followed her scent through the village to here.'

'Well, I don't think there is any reason to all sleep out here. Should we head back to the lodge?' Leslie said. 'It looks like they are staying the night.'

'Elephants would rather be somewhere safe when it gets dark than in a strange place,' Rodger said. 'It's nice that they chose this as their safe spot.'

'Mum, can I stay? Please? I want to make sure the leopard doesn't come back,' Joss said.

Stephen said. 'What if I said he's long gone? I heard from Mum that you guys did a great job of scaring him off with your singing.'

Joss laughed, snorting through his nose. 'Please?'

'Please, Daddy?' Courtney asked.

'I'll stay, too,' said Peta. 'I'd like to watch through the night in case they leave.'

'Joss, you can stay if the girls are staying,' Stephen said.

Rodger smiled. 'I'll stay with them. Tsessebe has been out with them all day. He needs some sleep.'

'Yippee!' Joss said a bit loudly, and the matriarch turned her head to look at him as if in disgust that he was disturbing their baby.

'I'll be back later with some dinner and hot chocolate. Be good and listen to Uncle Rodger,' Leslie said and kissed the top of Joss's head.

'Take care,' Stephen said.

'We will,' Peta said.

Stephen, Leslie, Bongani and Tsessebe climbed out of the stable on the side furthest from the elephants and made their way quietly back to the lodge.

Joss felt the touch on his head and then heard Ringo whine.

He was instantly awake.

The matriarch was standing next to Ndhlovy, and it was her trunk that had reached out to Joss.

'Uncle Rodger,' he whispered.

'I saw,' Rodger said, and he sat up so that the matriarch could see he was now awake as well.

'What's happening?' Peta asked quietly.

'The matriarch woke me up with her trunk,' Joss said.

The elephant moved off, but Ndhlovy stayed, her little trunk trying to touch Joss through the stable.

'I think she needs food,' Joss said. 'She's asking for her milk.' He put his hand out, and Ndhlovy wound her trunk around his hand.

'I'll make some,' Rodger said as he moved to the side of the stable to exit. The matriarch took another few steps back as he climbed out and made his way to the tack room, facing the herd the whole time.

Ringo, still inside the stable, licked Ndhlovy's trunk. The matriarch stepped forward, her big ears flapping, her trunk up, threatening.

'Ringo, heal!' Joss said.

Ringo shot inside the stable and sat next to Joss.

The matriarch backed off again.

Joss slowly began to climb out of the stable.

'Joss, no. It's dangerous!' Peta said.

'Fine,' he said, staying inside. Still touching Ndhlovy's trunk, he kept his front to the wooden fence. He slid along towards the open stable. Ndhlovy walked with him on the outside while Ringo was a silent shadow on the inside.

The matriarch stayed where she was, adjusting her position to watch him.

Once he was at Ndhlovy's stable, he walked further inside, and Ndhlovy followed. He turned her around to face the open door then put only the middle pole across to keep her in, or the matriarch out if need be.

Ringo leapt up and gave Ndhlovy kisses. She ran her trunk over his back, and he whined loudly, his whole body rocking from side to side with his tail whipping around furiously.

The matriarch rumbled, and Joss smiled. 'We won't hurt her, Mrs Elephant. We're trying to help save her.'

Rodger climbed back into the stables with Peta close behind him. Each held a bottle.

Ndhlovy lifted her trunk as Rodger passed Joss the milk and he put it in her mouth. She started drinking her bottle.

'Guess she's hungry again. Look how fast she's drinking,' Joss said.

Peta smiled. 'I can't believe that the matriarch woke you up to give Ndhlovy milk.' She took her turn to feed Ndhlovy.

Courtney came into the stable. Climbing over the pole, she rubbed her eyes. 'Hey, how come no one woke me up?'

'The matriarch touched me with her trunk to wake me, and she let us take Ndhlovy to feed her again. She was so hungry; she guzzled her first bottle so fast. She's slowing down now.' Joss patted the baby elephant on her shoulder.

'That's so sweet.' Courtney scratched behind Ndhlovy's ear. 'I'm so glad we got to touch her again and give her hugs.'

Rodger said, 'I think Stephen and I were right. They need some food to get the milk supply up before they take off into the bush again.'

'You think they are going to stay here?' Peta asked.

'I hope they stay around in the area. Let's see what happens in the next few hours,' Rodger said.

When Ndhlovy had finished her milk, she went to the door. She wrapped her trunk around the pole and tried to move it as the matriarch had done, but it wouldn't budge.

'Okay girl, you can go back to your family, but come back if you need more milk.' He slid the pole out, and Ndhlovy walked back to the matriarch, causing Ringo to whine.

The matriarch stroked Ndhlovy with her trunk. Ndhlovy moved back to where she'd been earlier and lay down again. The old elephant turned her back to the baby, facing her tusks outward. Like a wagon lager of the old pioneers, the adult elephants continued to protect the babies as they slept.

The pink sun filtered through the mopani trees as the fish eagles' haunting call serenaded the sunrise. The "kip-kip" sound of African skimmers competed with the noisy jacana and darters as they spread their wings to dry off in the early morning, eager to catch breakfast from the waters of the lake.

The elephants walked west, out of the camp towards the moringa grove again, only this time, little Ndhlovy accompanied them.

Joss watched as the last big cow left their stable area. Her tail swished back and forth, the hairy tip a natural flyswatter already chasing the pests away so early in the morning. He sighed loudly.

'Do you think they'll leave now that they have taken their baby?'

'I think she'll be back,' Rodger said. 'I don't think one extra meal for One-tusk is enough to get her milk supply up. I think we'll see the elephants again before nightfall.'

'I hope so,' said Peta. 'I don't think I'm quite ready to let that little one go yet. She's so beautiful. But that matriarch last night ... Wow.'

They all stood watching the spot where the elephants had disappeared into the bush.

'They're already gone,' said Joss as Leslie, Stephen, Bongani and Tsessebe reached the stable area.

'We know. We were watching with the binoculars,' Stephen said.

'The matriarch woke me to feed Ndhlovy during the

night, and you know what, Mum? It was like she knew that One-tusk didn't have enough milk because she asked us to feed Ndhlovy again.'

Leslie looked at Rodger who nodded.

'The Kenyans said that they've had animals arrive at their facility with poison arrows and spears in them as if knowing that they can come for help because they have the babies there. But to see it happen was a unique experience.'

'Dad,' Peta said, 'it was *amazing*.'

'And you left me to sleep,' Courtney said glaring at Peta.

'You woke up for the feeding. It's not like you missed everything,' Peta said.

'It's wonderful that you both got to experience this with Joss,' Rodger said.

'Are you going to stay with them again today, Tsessebe?' Joss asked.

Tsessebe nodded.

'Hey, Dad,' Peta called. 'Can I go with Tsessebe and track the elephants today on foot instead of hanging around here?'

Rodger turned towards Peta. Torn between an immediate "No, it's too dangerous" and seeing her as she truly was—eighteen and independent, but still wanting her father's permission. He couldn't refuse her.

'Yes, and I think I'll join you too.'

'Awesome. I can't remember when I last had a full day in the bush with you,' Peta said as she walked back to the stables.

He was still for a moment, then shook his head. He didn't want her anywhere near the wild adult herd, especially on the first day that Ndhlovy was with them, but he couldn't hold her back. She was enchanted by the elephants, and he understood her passion. He'd seen it in Helene, and to even attempt to curb it in his daughter would be useless. She was too much "their" child. The best parts of Helene and the most stubborn parts of him.

'Come down to the lodge and grab some food and water to take with you,' Leslie said.

'Can I come too?' Courtney asked.

'And me?' Joss joined in.

'Guess it's a yes all round,' Rodger said, 'if your dad says it's okay, Joss.'

'I can't very well say no if the girls are going, now can I?' But Stephen was laughing. 'I thought I knew you. Guess I was wrong. I thought for sure you'd say no.'

'I meant to, but somehow it came out a yes,' Rodger admitted. 'Just wait till Joss is a teenager, Stephen, then I'll be the one laughing at you. They turn the world upside down and over again.'

The elephant herd had browsed their way to the moringa grove, and they had stayed in the green trees all morning. Eating the leaves, seeds and pods.

'Aunty Leslie told me this grove was here when they built the lodge,' Peta said, 'but she expanded it and trims it regularly so that the village nearby can have access to the leaves.'

'That's no surprise.' Rodger said. 'Most of the safari lodges sink a lot of money back into the local communities to help the people.'

'Can you guys talk about something other than trees?' Courtney said.

'Sure,' Rodger said. 'How about the animals who eat them? Notice any other spoor around?'

'Jumbo,' Joss said. 'Mum normally freaks when the elephants visit and eat her trees. They eat the pods and leaves, and then they strip the bark off the trees before they leave. She doesn't like it when they do that.'

'You mean like this herd is doing?' Rodger asked.

'This is different—she knows these elephants. She hasn't complained as far as I've heard,' Joss said.

They watched as One-tusk broke another tree in half, trimming it down in size.

'Just as well they grow fast,' Rodger said.

'And all that elephant dung is free fertiliser,' Tsessebe said.

'*Ewwww*,' Courtney said.

Rodger patted her on the shoulder. 'As long as they recover. That's what we want for your Aunty Leslie.'

Gardening was one thing he'd never understood, and although Helene had attempted to have a few roses in their garden at Matusadona, they had simply kept to grass in the end ... it was easier. Well, grass in the wet when it rained and a dust bowl when there was none. Leslie had given a few of her propagated moringa plants to Helene, and the garden boy at the park had managed to keep them alive. But the elephants and all the browsing wild game that came into the area would take a nibble if they got a chance.

'It's amazing. It's as if that matriarch knew those trees were here, and she brought One-tusk to them to help her,' Rodger said. 'Look, the matriarch's moving away from the trees. Bet you they're going to cool down in the lake.'

'No way am I betting with you, Dad. You always win,'

Courtney said as they got up and wandered through the bush following the small herd.

The lake's water was dark, and despite knowing it was cool, no human swam at the water's edge for fear of a crocodile striking. Hippos grunted a little offshore as they hid from the sun in the water, only their ears and noses sticking out. One yawned, showing its huge yellow teeth, and then splashed into the water before disappearing on a dive.

On the shoreline, less than four hundred metres away, the herd had moved into the water to bathe, getting some relief from the heat of the midday sun. Surrounded by the older elephants, Ndhlovy went in and splashed around.

Joss laughed. 'Look at her. She's so healthy and loving the water.'

Rodger nodded. 'You two did good there, Joss, taking a chance on her—you and Bongani.'

'Thanks, Uncle Rodger,' Joss said, then he began laughing again as Ndhlovy threw herself down and whipped her trunk through the water.

They watched in silence as the elephants came out and then proceeded to take a sand bath on the shoreline, throwing it all over themselves.

The elephants continued to browse on the sweet grasses at the lake's edge, making their way away from the lodge toward Binga. The humans followed at a safe distance, all the time making sure they were downwind of the animals. Even though they knew the humans were there to help, Rodger wouldn't take any chance they might turn on them in the wild.

Then they moved around and began walking east again towards the lodge.

Tsessebe said, 'I think they are going to head back to the stable now. I saw Ndhlovy trying to drink from One-tusk again, and she does not seem to be getting anything.'

Rodger said, 'At the pace they walk, they should get there before sundown. I think we should cut across and arrive there before them, make sure everything is waiting at the stables again when they come in.'

'And what if they don't come to the stables?' Joss asked.

'It's a chance we take. Or we can continue following to see exactly where they go,' Rodger said.

'No. My feet are tired. I'm happy to take a shortcut,' Joss said, and they followed Tsessebe as he found a game path leading east through the bushes towards home.

CHAPTER 7
THE GIFTS

On Christmas morning, the girls rushed in to their dad's room still in their pyjamas. It was dark outside, and yet they had an excitement about them that only Christmas could bring.

'Dad, wake up. It's Christmas day!' Courtney hopped into his bed next to him on one side.

'Move over, Dad. She wouldn't let me sleep,' Peta said.

He smiled as he wiggled across into the middle, and Peta climbed in on the other side.

'Dad, look what Santa left in my stocking.' Courtney showed him a silver wrapped box. 'I wanted to open it with you like we used to do with Mum, but Peta didn't want to get out of bed.'

'I had a late night with Ndhlovy last night,' Peta said sleepily, but Rodger noticed that she also clutched her silver wrapped box with its silver ribbon.

'Well, open it,' he said.

Courtney ripped the paper apart and opened the hinged box. He smiled, knowing what was inside. He and Helene had spent hours on these presents when they had visited Bulawayo for her last appointment ... the day they'd been told nothing more could be done other than making as many memories together as they could.

'Wow,' Courtney said. 'Peta, you have to open your present!'

Suddenly very awake, Peta sat up and carefully removed the bow. Then she picked at the tape and slid the paper off.

Rodger laughed, looking skywards. Helene had predicted precisely how the girls would each open their presents.

Peta lifted her ring from the box. 'Oh Dad.' It was a thick silver band with chips of almost violet stone inlaid in the shape of a heart. And inside, engraved in tiny letters, were the words:

"Forever in our hearts ~ Dad & Mum."

Courtney leaned over Rodger and said to Peta, 'Look at mine. My heart's red.'

'That's because your birthstone is ruby and Peta's is tanzanite,' Rodger said. 'Your mum and I picked these out for you. She wanted you girls to have them this Christmas. And for you both to know that you are forever in her heart, even if she isn't here, and that you're also always in mine. Even when I get grumpy.' He smiled softly. 'When I miss your mum, all I need to do is look at the two of you, and I see her. In your smiles, in your eyes. She's always with us.'

'*Awww*, Dad,' Peta said and wrapped her arms around him.

Courtney did the same.

'Happy Christmas to the best daughters any dad could ask for.' Rodger held onto both of them.

'Can we open the other presents under the tree?' Courtney asked.

'When everyone's awake,' Rodger said.

At that moment, there was a knock on the door.

'You guys up yet?' Joss asked.

Courtney ran to open the door for him.

'Thanks, Dad,' Peta said. 'I love that you both had something to do with this Christmas present … that you and Mum were thinking so far ahead.'

'We had so much planned, so many places we wanted to take you girls, so many things we wished we could have given you, but these rings were the last thing that we were able to get you two together.'

'We'll always treasure them,' Peta said.

'Come on, you two. Joss said that Aunty Leslie and Uncle Stephen are up already and that there are hot mince pies for breakfast!' Courtney grabbed her box off the bed. She plucked the trinket from the velvet, pushed her ring onto her middle finger, and then ran out after Joss.

'Dad, what did Mum get you for Christmas?' Peter asked. 'Did you guys plan that, too?'

'Actually, yes. Look in the drawer next to you. I'm not sure how practical it will be, but I couldn't say no to her.'

Peta opened the drawer, took out a jewellery box the same as hers and Courtney's, and opened it. Inside, she found three gold bands intertwined with one of their names engraved on each—*Helene, Courtney* and *Peta.*

'The three loves of my life,' Rodger said, slipping the intertwined bands onto his right ring finger.

'Oh Dad, that's beautiful,' Peta said as she hugged him again.

'Come on. Best get going to join the others because you know Courtney and Joss. They'll rip into everything if they have half a chance and there are a few presents under that tree for you,' Rodger said.

Peta laughed and climbed out the bed. 'Race you,' she said.

Then, before giving him a chance to respond, she dashed out of the room and up to the main house.

Boxing Day arrived. The clouds had gathered during the night, and the dark sky threatened rain. The smell of it hung heavy in the air, and the elephants were restless.

They'd flattened the moringa trees in the grove. There was nothing left except silver stalks pointing skywards, and they'd eaten all the lucerne and hay that the lodge had to spare.

Joss knew that the day was coming soon when the elephants would leave. Ndhlovy was feeding less and less from him, sleeping out all night and having one feed early in the morning before browsing further and further with her herd. But he still loved every minute with her. For two days now, he hadn't had his wake-up touch on his head from the matriarch.

Ndhlovy didn't need him anymore.

Except for the night before Christmas when they had all been told to sleep inside in their own beds, they had pretty much slept out every night with the elephants. He sniffed his sleeping bag and knew it smelt like elephant. Everything did. Despite Mosman cleaning out their dung every day in the wheelbarrow and throwing it out, Joss could still smell that they had made their home near the stables.

But he didn't care. His elephant was now fit and becoming naughty. Getting bored with being where she was, Ndhlovy was starting to explore. Early one morning, she'd followed Joss down to the house when he went to brush his teeth and change clothes. Only his mum warning him not to bring her onto the deck had made him turn around, because he hadn't noticed that One-tusk was right behind her.

He'd tried giving her a ball to play with, but that had been quickly popped, as had the spare soccer ball, his basketball and even both his rugby balls.

Rodger sat with Joss and his daughters, having had the night shift with them. 'You know they'll leave soon. With the return of the guests and the extra human activity, the matriarch will move her herd back into the Chizarira. One-tusk doesn't need the extra feed anymore. The rains have been constant, and the new grasses are growing. Water's pooling in the rivers, so the time is coming for them to go back into the bush.'

'I know,' Joss said. 'And I'm glad, but I will miss them. All of them.'

'Me too,' said Peta.

'And me,' said Courtney.

The matriarch came towards the stable fence. She stood silently for a while then a low rumble came as she extended her trunk to Joss. He reached out one hand without thinking.

She touched the tip of her trunk into his hand.

'Go slowly, Joss,' Rodger warned.

She moved slightly to the left, reached for Peta and repeated the gesture.

'She's saying goodbye, isn't she Dad?' Peta said. 'They're leaving.'

'I think so,' Rodger said.

The matriarch touched Courtney's hand, and then she turned and walked away, stopping before the path that led east, the path they had arrived on that first morning. One-tusk approached the stable. She let out a low rumble, and Ndhlovy came to her. Ndhlovy put her trunk through the stable and Joss wrapped his arms around her trunk. He stepped forward and put his head against hers through the wooden stable side. One-tusk rumbled again, and Peta and Courtney stepped forward to touch her and say goodbye.

Ringo whined. He went forward and licked at Ndhlovy's trunk as it came down to caress him, and then he barked twice.

Then One-tusk turned and walked away. Ndhlovy stayed for only a moment and then ran after her mother.

The other elephants followed as the matriarch began her slow path east. Ringo was howling a slow lament in farewell to his friend, expressing the loss of something precious.

Tears ran down Peta's cheeks. Unchecked they dripped onto her shirt. She sniffed and then turned to her dad as huge sobs tore through her.

'At least she isn't alone, Dad. At least her family came to look for her, and she isn't an orphan. But it's so hard to see her go,' she said, between gasps for breath.

Rodger held her, and Courtney came to his side. 'You think they're really gone, Dad?'

'I do,' he said, bringing her into the hug. 'Joss, quickly go fetch Tsessebe. He can follow them. Make sure they get back to Chizarira without any troubles.'

Joss ran towards the rondavels of the guesthouse to where Tsessebe was staying. Ringo bounded after him.

'Bongani! Tsessebe!' he called as he ran. 'They're leaving. You have to follow them!'

'Well, that will wake the whole camp. That wasn't quite what I meant,' Rodger said under his breath.

'Yeah, Dad. With Joss, sometimes you have to say exactly what you mean,' Peta said. She sniffed, and he kissed the top of her head.

'You two okay? I know it's sad to see Ndhlovy go, but it's a good sad. She's with her mum and her herd.'

'I know, and I'm good,' Peta said. 'But it's a long way back to the Chizarira from here on foot.'

Rodger smiled. 'That it is, and we'll leave Tsessebe to do this part. There are too many wild animals out there, poachers, villagers—you stay with us here. When they're safe again, Tsessebe will make contact, and we can fetch him, wherever he is. By plane, by boat. This is part of Ndhlovy's journey you girls can't go on.'

'But Dad …' Peta protested.

'Not up for discussion, Peta. There are too many risks,' Rodger said.

'I don't agree with you, but okay.' She was silent for a moment. 'If you went too, then we could go.'

'No. One or two people are enough. They don't need a whole entourage following through the bush. We would only cause trouble for the herd. Let them go. Let that matriarch protect her family, like she has been doing for many,

many years, and leave them be. Our help isn't needed anymore.'

Peta stood next to him and sniffed. 'I don't want this time with you to be over, Dad. It's been so great being here, having you around all the time.'

'Peta,' Rodger said. 'I'll always be here. I'm not going anywhere. Come on, lift your ring up and make a fist. Courtney, you do the same—'

The girls lifted their hands. Rodger copied them, and then he brought their hands closer with his left hand, and their three fists touched. 'I'm your dad and I'm not going anywhere. I'll be here till the end. You girls are stuck with me.'

Peta smiled through her tears.

Courtney said, 'So that's a definite no, we can't go with Tsessebe?'

'It's a no, Courtney,' Rodger said.

'And if Joss goes?' Courtney asked.

'I don't think he'll go either, not if I know Leslie and Stephen. But that's their choice. Their family. And each family has to do what's right for them. They'll muddle through, just like we do.'

'We don't muddle, Dad,' Peta said. 'We splash through in style!'

They all laughed as they began to walk hand-in-hand down the path, east towards the rising pink sun peeking through the dark clouds.

GLOSSARY

Bateleur Eagle – (Terathopius Ecaudatus) A colourful eagle species found in open savanna country and woodland (thornveld) within Sub-Saharan Africa; it also occurs in south-west Arabia.

Chete Safari Area – Situated on the shores of Lake Kariba between the Senkwe and Muenda rivers. It is a controlled hunting area and one of Zimbabwe's most rugged concessions.

Chipangali – A wildlife rescue refuge in Bulawayo, Zimbabwe.

Chizarira National Park – A large national park found in Northern Zimbabwe.

Matusadona National Park – A large game park in Northern Zimbabwe.

Skabenga – (*ska-beng-ga*) General Southern African phrase used to describe a criminal or a shady person.

TTL – Tribal Trust Lands. Now referred to as Communal Lands. Small-scale and subsistence farming are the principal economic activities in communal lands. The farms of communal lands are traditionally unfenced and communal lands have a resident traditional African Chief who oversees the community.

Velskoene/Veldskoene/Velskoen – Bush shoes. Suede leather ankle boots, usually worn without socks. (Afrikaans)

If you enjoyed The Avoidable Orphan, please turn over for an extract of T.M. Clark's bestseller
Child of Africa

ACKNOWLEDGEMENTS

Thank you Michael North Imagery, for the stunning original cover photo used on the previous edition. More of his beautiful images can be found on his Facebook page

CHILD OF AFRICA

CHAPTER 1

DREAMERS

Kajaki Hydroelectric Scheme, Afghanistan, 2008

The four-kilometre-long convoy snaked into the Kajaki Hydroelectric Plant. Joss Brennan watched the turbines arriving at the dam wall through his binoculars and wanted to dance around, even though he was just one of five thousand troops who had played their part in protecting Turbine T2. But celebrations would have to wait.

Seven sections of turbine, each weighing between twenty and thirty tons, had been transported the final one hundred and eighty kilometres from Kandahar air base, through the Helmand Valley and the desert and finally up to Kajaki Lake. Some optimist had painted holy slogans and an Afghan flag on the containers to try to dig deep into the patriotism the locals had for their country—T2 belonged to the people. It seemed to have worked, because the heavy convoy had arrived at its destination. The people of Afghanistan would soon have two working turbines, creating power and bringing them electricity.

Chinook helicopters flew overhead, loud as they passed low, sweeping the area.

Ten days of hell were almost over.

The eighty-ton crane was the next piece of equipment to come to a halt. As important as the segments themselves, it would help the engineers lift the parts off the trucks. Each minute the sections sat around was a minute longer that the troops had to protect them from the Taliban.

Joss adjusted his binoculars and looked further up the hill, following the line carefully, looking for anything out of place in the rugged terrain. The word in the barracks was that almost two hundred insurgents had been cleared on the route through and around the dam. He hoped that was true and they were unable to return, but there were always those who, like snakes, slipped through the cracks to come back to bite their butts another day.

He scanned the compound in a grid pattern, making sure no one would threaten this precious cargo, not after the epic mission they had just accomplished. This was his job, the sniper, the tracker, the spotter in his company. Who knew that watching the animals in Africa all those years ago would be such good practice for hunting the enemy when he became a British Marine Commando? Who would have known that the hours spent with his father and Bongani in the bush, learning the skills of a hunter, would help him be the ultimate marine?

Joss went over the grid a second time. 'Check two o'clock on the ridge. Shadow protruding beyond the wall,' he said into his mic. 'Definitely something moving in the compound.' But in the next moment, the shadow had gone, and all that remained was the edge of the wall.

'Affirmative. Suspect unfriendlies,' Mitch's Australian twang answered.

'Don't jump to conclusions, might be the locals. Eleventh troop mobilise. Sweep compound,' Lieutenant Colonel Johnathan Tait-Markham—Tank to his friends—ordered over the coms.

After a quick glance at the convoy still rolling in, Joss packed his binoculars. Mitch put his hand out to help him up.

'Crack on, we have a compound to clear,' came Tank's voice.

Joss bent and ran with Mitch just a few steps behind. The stones at their feet slid loosely until their boots gripped the baked surface beneath.

They reached the compound and were soon hot-footing it along the mud wall. Joss remembered this village well—they had previously cleared an IED from exactly where he walked now. They'd returned a few times since the initial clearing, but that didn't mean that there were no more IEDs. Insurgents could creep in at any time and rearm a place.

'Affix bayonets. Two break left, two break right,' Tank instructed.

Joss saw Mitch and Tank break left. He rounded the corner of the same hole they had blasted in the mud wall a few weeks back, Cricket, one of his fellow marines, with him. He heard the wasp sounds as bullets flew close to his head. He hit the dirt and rolled for cover.

'Contact. Contact,' Tank shouted into the mic.

Crawling after Cricket, Joss slipped into a room. They swept it quickly.

'Clear,' Cricket said.

'Wait,' Joss said as he saw a carpet hanging on the wall move. He indicated with his head towards it. Outside he could hear the shallow *pop-pop* sound of the insurgents' AKs and the deeper sounds of their own rifles.

'Joss, where are you?' Tank called. 'We need a sniper.'

'Clearing this—'

He got no further as the carpet came to life. Someone was screaming, and the whole thing came down, exposing an insurgent with his gun raised.

Cricket and Joss shot him down in a hail of bullets.

Joss approached the body. He kicked the AK-47 away, and looked at the man.

Correction.

Boy.

Joss knelt down and checked for a pulse, but there was none. He was relieved and sad.

No more than fourteen, the boy had only the wispy beginning of a moustache. His black turban still clung tightly to his head. He looked too young to be carrying a weapon and trying to kill them. He should still be in school.

This was someone's son. Someone's child who might not have wanted to be a soldier.

Or worse, this could have been a child who chose this path, thinking it was his shortcut to glory in the afterlife.

Joss swallowed. It was survival—if they hadn't shot him, they would be the ones lying on the floor. 'Dead,' he told Cricket, and together they moved out of the room, to help the rest of the troop.

* * *

The stone chips pitted Joss's face, flicked up by bullets that were unnervingly accurate and close. One whistled past his ear. Joss adjusted his scope. 'Bogie at three o'clock.'

He squeezed the trigger.

The man's head jerked back. Joss slid the bolt of his rifle, ejecting the shell and loading another.

'Three o'clock,' he said as he shot the next man who was keeping his troop pinned down.

Again he reloaded.

Taking a breath, he looked for the third insurgent he'd seen. He had gone to ground.

'Lost visual,' he informed Mitch.

Mitch looked through his binoculars, scanning the small hill on the other side of the village. 'Four o'clock, blue-black turban. Behind a wall—must be a ledge beneath it that he's using.'

Joss adjusted his weapon and took aim at the designated place, even though he could see nothing there. The turban rose as the man wearing it peered over the ledge to check where his enemy had got to. Calmly, Joss fired, and the man dropped out of sight.

'Hit?' Mitch asked.

'Affirmative,' Joss said as he reloaded.

Mitch nodded. 'Bad angle, I couldn't be sure from here.'

The firing had stopped. The silence that followed any fight was always deafening. The wait for the next shot terrifying in case it came right for you.

'Any more?' Mitch asked.

Joss took a deep breath and swept his scope over the side of the hill. A single goat nibbled at non-existent grass. 'Wait ... look left of the goat.'

Mitch focused on the goat, then left. 'Bogie,' he affirmed. 'He has a rocket launcher.'

They saw the tip of the man's head, his arms outstretched to launch the deadly missile at them or at the precious convoy of trucks.

Joss took him down. The sound of the single shot was loud in the silence that had descended.

The goat bleated and tried to run away, but it seemed tethered to the insurgent. Panicked, it bleated some more.

'Continue to clear area,' Tank shouted over the coms and the men came out from where they had taken cover to sweep the village.

'If we let that goat go, it'll lead us to where they came from,' Joss said. 'Find their base.'

'Negative,' Tank replied. 'It's getting late; we pass that on to the American troops to follow up. I'm in contact with HQ, and they have a command passing us in ten minutes. Check fire. Friendlies approaching from behind.'

Joss watched as the American marines chatted to Tank on their way through. He pointed to the goat, and their leader nodded. Then they were off, along with the goat, over the small hill and out for their night patrol.

Joss's company gathered and headed towards their temporary barracks, spirits high, adrenaline levels beginning to lower. Joss grinned. This was what he had been born to do—wear his green beret and serve the greater good, just like his grandfather. Help people who were unable to stand up to tyranny. Fight for freedom and justice when those around couldn't.

Tonight he would pen another letter to Courtney, like he always did when something significant took place, then he would watch it burn, as was regulation. He would rewrite it when he got back to England, after he was out of the desert, a more sanitised version. An emotionless version that would never depict the true horrors they experienced out here, or the simple joys of just waking up, knowing that you had achieved something amazing.

It didn't matter that Courtney didn't write back often; he just wanted her to know he was okay out here in the world beyond Africa. He kept the letters he'd received from her in England, and any that he received while on the front line he would read, commit to memory, then burn so that the enemy would not get their hands on them.

Letters to his best friend, and phone calls to Bongani, his lodge manager, were his only connection to his home in Zimbabwe now that his parents were gone.

Click here to keep reading Child of Africa

ABOUT THE AUTHOR

Zimbabwean-born T.M. Clark combines her passion for storytelling, different cultures and wildlife with her love for the wild in her multicultural books. Writing for adults and children, she has been nominated for a Queensland Literary Award and is a Children's Book Council Notable. When not killing her fans and hiding their bodies (all in the name of literature), Tina Marie coordinates the CYA Conference (www.cyaconference.com), providing professional development for new and established writers and illustrators, and is the co-presenter at Writers at Sea (www.WritersAtSea.com.au). She loves mentoring emerging writers, eating chocolate biscuits and collecting books for creating libraries in Papua New Guinea.

Visit T.M. Clark at tmclark.com.au or

facebook.com / tmclarkauthor

x.com / tmclark_author

instagram.com / tmclark_author

amazon.com / stores / author / B018N3D2QY

bookbub.com / authors / t-m-clark

goodreads.com / tmclark

linkedin.com / in / t-m-clark

mastodon.au / @tmclark

pinterest.com / TMClark_Author

tiktok.com / @tmclark_author

threads.net / @tmclark_author

ALSO BY T.M. CLARK

ADULT NOVELS

- Child of Africa
- Cry of the Firebird
- My Brother-But-One
- Nature of the Lion
- Shooting Butterflies
- Tears of the Cheetah
- The Avoidable Orphan
- Song of the Starlings

PICTURE BOOKS

- Slowly! Slowly!
- Quickly! Quickly!

Printed in Great Britain
by Amazon